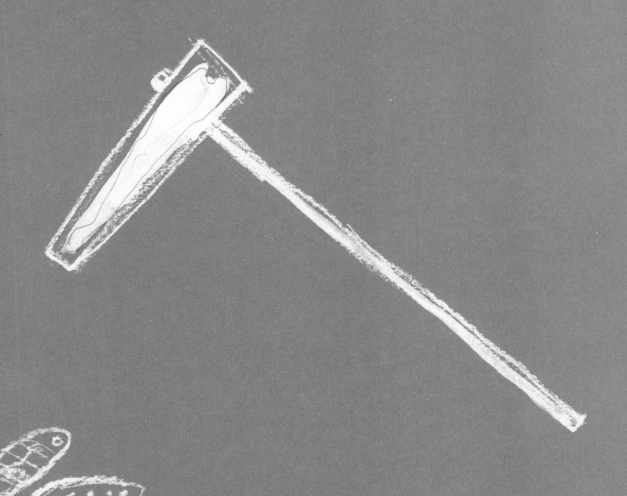

149 9608

Story © 1985 by Tamizo Shibano
Illustrations © 1985 by Bunshu Iguchi

First Printing 1985

Heian International, Inc.
P.O. Box 1013
Union City, CA 94587

Originally published by Froebel-Kan Ltd., Tokyo

Translated by D.T. Ooka

ISBN: 0-89346-247-0

Printed in Japan

The Old Man who made the Trees Bloom

Hanasaka Jijii

retold by Tamizo Shibano
illustrated by Bunshu Iguchi

Heian

Long, long ago a very kind and honest old couple lived next door to a very mean and greedy old couple. The kind old man and woman were very poor and had no children, but they had a big, white dog named Shiro. They loved Shiro very much and treated him like their own child. Whenever the old man went to the forest to gather wood, Shiro went to keep him company. At night, Shiro was a wonderful watchdog that guarded the kind old couple's house and fields.

The greedy old couple had no children and no pets. Whenever they saw Shiro, they would yell at him, throw sticks and stones at him, and chase Shiro away.

One day, Shiro began to bark loudly and dig under a tree in the kind old man's back yard.

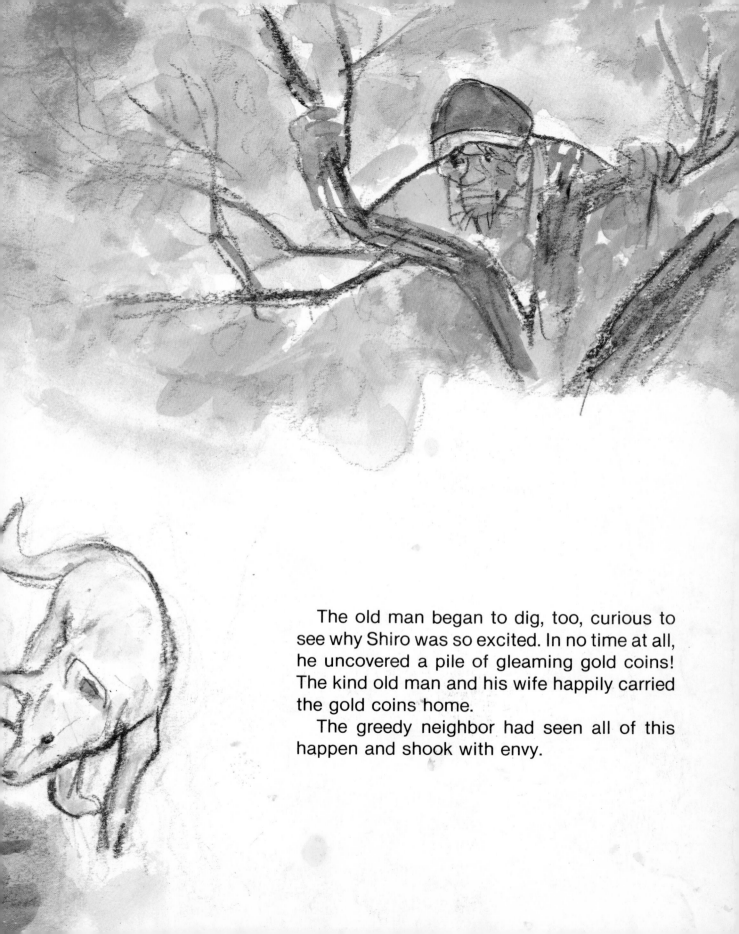

The old man began to dig, too, curious to see why Shiro was so excited. In no time at all, he uncovered a pile of gleaming gold coins! The kind old man and his wife happily carried the gold coins home.

The greedy neighbor had seen all of this happen and shook with envy.

The next day, the greedy old man came to the kind old couple and very politely asked if he could borrow Shiro for a while. The kind old man could not refuse, so the greedy neighbor tied a rope around Shiro's neck and dragged the unhappy dog to his back yard.

"Ha! Now I'll find my own pile of gold!" rejoiced the greedy old man. He tied a rope so tightly around Shiro that Shiro began to scratch at the ground in pain. The greedy old man pushed Shiro aside and began to dig. But instead of gold, he uncovered an evil, foul-smelling pile of garbage, broken dishes, bottles, snakes, and frogs!

The greedy neighbor was so angry that he killed Shiro and buried him under the tree. When Shiro's kind master came to ask if he could take Shiro home, the greedy man said, "Bah! That lazy good-for-nothing dog? I killed him and buried him under that tree!"

The kind old man wept sadly. He cut down the tree where Shiro was buried and took it home. From the tree he made a mortar and pestle.

"Mother, I've made the mortar and pestle. Let's use it to make some of Shiro's favorite millet cakes. Then we can put the cakes on his grave," said the kind old man.

But when they began to pound the millet, a most amazing thing happened! Bright, shiny gold coins began to fly out of the mortar! Again, the greedy neighbor watched it all...and again, he was filled with envy.

The greedy man came to the kind old couple, saying, "I feel so badly about killing Shiro—could I possibly borrow your mortar and pestle to make some millet cakes? I'd like to put them on his grave to apologize." Once more, the kind old couple could not refuse.

The greedy old neighbor gleefully carried the mortar and pestle home. But when he and his wife began to pound the millet, mud and garbage poured out of the mortar, making a smelly mess.

Furious, the greedy old man grabbed an axe, chopped up the mortar and pestle, and burned it. When the kind old man came to fetch his mortar and pestle, all he could take home were the ashes from his greedy neighbor's fireplace.

"Mother," said the kind old man, "these ashes are all we have left of Shiro. They will be good for the trees." As he began to scatter the ashes, the bare branches of the cherry and plum trees burst into bloom. It was a miracle, for spring was still very far away.

Delighted with the beauty surrounding them, the kind old couple carefully put the rest of the ashes away. Soon afterwards, an Imperial messenger came. He said, "The Emperor has heard that you can make bare trees bloom. He wants to see you work your magic at the palace."

So at the palace, before the Emperor, the Empress, and all the lords and ladies, the kind old man climbed up into the branches of a cherry tree. As soon as he scattered the ashes, the tree was covered with pink and white clouds of flowers. The Emperor was so pleased that he gave the kind old man the title of "The Old Man Who Makes the Trees Bloom" and sent him home with a huge pile of gold and other treasures.

Having seen all this, the greedy old man ran to his fireplace and scooped out the rest of the ashes. He hurried to the Emperor's palace and told him that he was the real "Old Man Who Makes the Trees Bloom" and that the kind old man was just his student. "If you are the first 'Old Man Who Makes the Trees Bloom,' then you must be better than your student," said the Emperor. "Please, show us your magic."

The greedy old man climbed up into a tree and began to throw the ashes. But his ashes remained ashes, and not a blossom appeared anywhere. The old man frantically scattered more and more ashes, until some fell on the Emperor and his court, dirtying their beautiful robes and blinding their eyes. The Emperor was furious! "You are not the 'Old Man Who Makes the Trees Bloom'," roared the Emperor, "you are an impostor!" The greedy old man was tied up and taken to prison.

Unlike their greedy neighbor, the kind old couple continued to live unselfishly and happily, always grateful to their good dog Shiro.

AFTERWORD
by Professor Keigo Seki

    This fable, like many other traditional Japanese folk tales, illustrates good and bad, greed and unselfishness in the natures of the two neighbors. It teaches children the virtues of being good and unselfish while showing that evil and greed do not pay. This tale also incorporates traditional beliefs about the dead, as the dead dog Shiro's spirit endows the tree over his grave with magical properties. Thus the mortar made from the tree over Shiro's grave fills with gold coins and the ashes turn into blossoms on the trees. Symbolizing the rebirth of life after death, the ashes turn into cherry blossoms and then cherries.